Cupid's Shot

A High Five Novella
Book #2

By Serena Pier

*To all the girls who dream of a buff dom in angel wings,
Aaron Olson has arrived.*

Content Warning

Alcohol Consumption, Anxiety, Profanity, Sexually
Explicit Content

Reading Order

***High Five Novella* Series:**

Santa's Coming

Cupid's Shot

Shamrock Kisses

Prologue

Aaron

Friday, January 3rd

"You want me to what?" I ask, stunned with the Valentine's-themed idea from High Five's social media team. Staring at the laptop on the bar, I shake my head again, still in disbelief. *Angel wings?*

Nicholas, who bought the dive bar in Lake Geneva, Wisconsin at the end of last summer, is chuckling, sitting beside me. He gives my shoulder a squeeze. "It's only fair," he says, too amused for my liking. "You're the manager now."

When I took on more responsibility, I didn't think it would mean this.

"I've liked working at High Five more since you came around," I mutter, still side-eyeing him, "but these days ... the Santa suit you wore last month was child's play compared to what you're asking me to do now."

"What's the big deal?" Taylor, our twenty-something account manager, pipes up over the virtual meeting. "Give the people what they want," she encourages.

1

Nicholas's smile widens, and the urge to smack him grows. "You've got a fan club. Trust me, those wings will make the ladies go crazy."

I sigh, rubbing my temples as the image of myself shirtless in angel wings flashes before my eyes. I know exactly how this will go. If our Christmas pop-up event was any indication, this single's event will be packed—and the money will be good. Like, way beyond a regular weekend in February good.

Still. Angel wings?

Grabbing Nicholas's phone out of his hand, I stare down at the wings he wants to order. I look ridiculous already.

"No way," I protest, shaking my head. "At least the Santa suit gave you an in with Emily. Who will the wings attract for me ... besides all the regulars taking the opportunity to feel me up?"

Nicholas chuckles again, because of course, he knows I'm right. The local ladies—fun as they are—are going to have a field day. "You'll make a grand in tips, easy."

I huff, knowing just how right he is. "I have to wear these all night?"

"Yes," Taylor chimes in, the growing smirk on her face making me regret ever agreeing to this meeting. It was her idea after all to do the Christmas pop-up, and she's been running with these viral concepts ever since. I've got to admit she's good at her job. The bar's online following has exploded thanks to her, and for this being the off season, I'm making decent money. Usually the off season has me questioning if summer's busy season is enough to justify this job.

"And I have to take photos with people?" I ask, although I already know the answer.

"Only for one hour," Nicholas adds, like he's doing me a favor.

I cross my arms. "And I'm guessing these photos are what, supposed to go viral on TikTok?"

Taylor's nod is swift, like it's already a done deal. "Aaron mixing drinks, shirtless and in angel wings? Viral all day, every day. We agreed increasing the bar's presence ahead of summer was top priority, remember?"

Right. The TikTok thing. Part of me gets it—business is business—but the other part of me wonders what's next. Am I going to be a shirtless bartender during every holiday now?

I steal another glance at the wings on Nicholas's phone, and a thought hits me. "If you also wear wings that night," I say, leveling my gaze at him, "I'll do it."

Nicholas pauses for a second, his eyes narrowing before he smirks. "Done. It'll be a good excuse to lose my winter weight."

I shake my head with a laugh, my competitive side waking up. "Now you're making it a competition?"

"Game on," he challenges, leaning back on his barstool.

I cock my brow at him, ready for the challenge. "I won't touch a carb until it's showtime."

"We're settled then," Taylor says, practically bouncing in her chair. She's a little too excited about this. "Two Cupid bartenders and photos with Aaron as Cupid. Did you like our ideas about the drink specials?"

Our meeting continues with drink specials and hashtags, but I'm still reeling from the fact that I just agreed to wear angel wings, shirtless, for the Cupid's Crush event. What the hell have I gotten myself into?

1

Sarah

Saturday, February 8th

The last time all three of us were at High Five, Emily found a man. I doubt I'll get struck by Cupid's arrow tonight, but I'm hoping to find some banter and a free drink. Walking into the local dive bar, I spot Emily and Rachel already seated at a tall boy table.

"Where are your pants?" Emily's motherly tone scolds, seeing me approach.

"What?" I smile, bouncing to the techno version of a classic love song blaring through the speakers. The place is decked out—there's hardly an inch of ceiling left without red and pink streamers or heart-shaped decorations. "This is how all the girls online are dressing," I say, plopping down beside them. "I'm on trend."

"Do you at least have volleyball shorts under that sweat-shirt?" Emily squints at me.

Lifting up my oversized red crewneck sweater, I show them my red spandex shorts and spank my ass for effect.

"Another day, another grand entrance from Sarah."

Rachel laughs, shaking her head. "Those sunglasses are too cute, though!"

I smile, also loving my heart-shaped pink sunglasses.

"Where's your Valentine?" I ask Emily, thrilled she's finally dating again. She's still in the early stages of her relationship with Nicholas, and I really like him for her.

"Somewhere around here," she says, scanning the room. We all do, trying to spot him. The place looks like Cupid exploded—rose petals and heart-shaped candies on every table, tea lights flickering softly.

"He's not going to be jealous?" I tease. "You sitting unaccompanied at a single's event?"

"Please." Emily gives me a side eye. "I'm here to support you two single ladies and manage what I'm sure will be a growing line of suitors."

I open my mouth to respond, but instead, a weird noise escapes—almost a shrill squeal. "Since when does Aaron have abs like that?!"

Aaron, who we all know from growing up in Lake Geneva, Wisconsin, has been bartending at High Five for years. Tonight, he's shirtless, wearing angel wings, and rocking a drool-worthy V-shape that makes me want things I've never considered. His pants are slung low, just right. *When did this happen?* Lusting after him feels strange since I've known him since kindergarten.

"Well," Rachel starts slowly, her face looking like she's combing through all of her memories. "I've only seen him in one of those wrestling outfits when we were in school."

"It's called a singlet," I inform the girls. Aaron looks so different from when we were in high school, in a very good way.

"Didn't he wrestle at the lowest weight class?" Emily asks.

"Something like that." He didn't peak at eighteen, that's for sure. Aaron is jacked yet not beefy. He's at least sixty pounds heavier, which isn't saying much. "He was definitely under one hundred and twenty-five pounds, I remember that."

Aaron Olson is all fucking man now. And that's ... too weird. My pulse quickens. *Get a grip, Sarah. This is Aaron. The nice guy that helped tutor you so you'd pass calculus.* The more I stare at him, the more I feel like I'm crossing some invisible line I shouldn't even be near. I look at the drink menu, trying to distract myself. I may literally drool if I stare at Cupid any longer.

"I'm torn between The First Kiss and Head Over Heels," Rachel says after a moment.

"They have so many good cocktails for this event!" I manage to smile, pretending I'm not still distracted by the sight of Aaron.

"Shots for the ladies!" The server arrives with a tray of Jello shots. We all stare at them, hesitation flashing across our faces. I want to laugh. In our twenties, we would have screamed in excitement for Jello shots. Now, in our thirties, all I can think about is how shots are usually the gateway to a hangover.

"And you," the server points at me. "The 'hot girl with the legs.' These are from a secret admirer."

Rachel and Emily squeal in unison. "The hot girl with the legs!"

"Well, I've achieved one of tonight's goals." I smile with a growing smugness.

"And what's that?" Rachel presses.

"A free drink."

"So, who is it from?" I ask the server, curious now.

"I've been sworn to secrecy," she says with a wink.

"They're doing tons of promos tonight," Emily adds. "You can send a singing telegram—oh my God!" Her eyes widen, and she bursts out laughing. We all turn to see Nicholas behind the bar, also shirtless, wearing wings.

"Damn, Em." I laugh, picking my jaw up from the floor. "You have left out some major details about Santa."

She laughs, her face blushing. "I didn't know he would be wearing that."

"Nicholas sure goes all out for the holidays." Rachel laughs.

"You have no idea." Emily smirks.

Rachel sweeps her hair behind her shoulder, sitting up taller.

"Are you, like, peacocking?" I tease.

"I want a secret admirer too."

"Want me to call Aaron over here?" Emily asks. "I know he's single."

"Pass for me," Rachel says. "He's hot, but I'm in my husky era."

We giggle, but Emily's eyes land on me next. "What about you? Why not flirt with Aaron?"

"Aaron? No way."

"Because he's a local?" Rachel sasses. "Remember, you live here again."

"You're going to have to update your rule at some point." Emily squints at me.

"Nah. I have never dated a townie, and I never will."

"That rule made sense in high school," Rachel nudges me, "when you knew you were moving to Los Angeles."

"It still makes sense."

"But you live here now. You're back," Emily presses. "It's been what, almost a year since you've returned to the land of cheese?"

"You're all about supporting local, except when it comes to dating." Rachel chuckles, taking Emily's side.

I wave my hands—over this conversation. I never wanted to get trapped in this small town, yet now that I'm back after living on the west coast for over a decade … I like it. It's my home.

2

Aaron

There are a lot of regulars in this bar, but Sarah Anderson isn't one of them. She was always that cool, artsy girl in high school, the one who never really fit into the small-town mold. When she went off to California after graduation, it felt like the natural next step for her. Time flies. It's been nearly thirteen years since we graduated, and though I've heard she's been back in town, I haven't seen her much. The last time was a couple of months ago at our Christmas pop-up event.

I've always been intrigued by her. Back then, she had this effortless way about her—creative, bold, someone who wasn't afraid to be different. Meanwhile, I was the skinny kid on the wrestling team, and she's never given me the time of day. Not that I blame her. I never gave her a reason to.

Staring at her long, toned legs, I decide to take a page out of Nicholas's playbook. I'm going to use Cupid's magic to break the ice.

"Claire," I say, getting the new server's attention. "Send a round of Jello shots to Emily's table and tell the hot girl with the legs that they're from a secret admirer."

Watching Sarah for a moment, I find the heart-shaped sunglasses she's wearing ridiculous, but on her, they work. With her light blue eyes and long, dark brown hair, she's always been striking.

"You look so hot!" Karen, one of the regulars, interrupts my thoughts, practically panting as she leans against the bar.

I laugh, shaking a cocktail. "Thanks, Karen."

"I can't wait to get a photo with you later," she adds with a wink, enjoying the spectacle of me shirtless with these ridiculous angel wings.

I flash her a smile, grateful for the brief distraction. I missed seeing Sarah's reaction when the shots arrived at her table, but that's probably for the best. I don't need to over-think it. My mind starts wandering, though, thinking about what I could do next. Maybe something a little more personal.

Although, I can't get too distracted with all the orders flying in. I buzz the office, pressing the button under the bar. Nicholas has been hiding in there for way too long. I need his help with these drinks.

"And there he is," I tease as he finally emerges.

"We are never doing this again," he grumbles, tugging at the wings on his back. "This is so much worse than the Santa suit."

"Are you getting nervous about what Taylor's going to propose for St. Paddy's on our next call?"

"I'm Nicholas O'Malley. I have St. Paddy's covered."

"Good!" I sigh with relief. Looking around the crowded bar, I say, "This event might even be more successful than our Christmas pop up."

As Nicholas grabs printed drink orders, I pause for a moment. I've got an idea. *Something more thoughtful.*

I grab a cocktail glass and start mixing. A bit of gin, some lavender syrup, a splash of elderflower liqueur—something with an artistic flair, just like her. I choose a purple garnish, subtle but striking, and smile as I look at the finished product. It's got that creative edge that reminds me of her, something unique but not over the top.

"Claire," I call out again, handing her the drink. "Take this over to Legs, and don't tell her who it's from." I press my finger to my lips.

3

Sarah

"This is for Legs," the server says, placing a cocktail in front of me.

"That's beautiful!" Rachel swoons.

Taking my first sip, this drink is incredible. It's floral and light. My eyes instinctively scan the bar, searching for a clue, someone who might be watching me. No one's making eye contact. No one's giving off "secret admirer" vibes. *Is it the guy in the red bowling shirt?* I cringe at the thought. *Please, no.* Or maybe it's the guy pumping his fist by the DJ booth, lost in his own world. *Definitely not.*

"I'm going to go ask Aaron who bought me this drink," I inform the girls. My patience is running thin.

"Oh, come on!" Emily squints at me. "Let the fantasy play out a little."

"Nah. I need to know." I've never been known for being a patient person.

"What if it's him?" Rachel asks.

"Aaron?" I laugh. "It's not April Fool's Day."

"It would be impressive if it was him," Emily says. "The poor guy is slammed."

Sliding off the tall boy chair, I head toward the bar with my eyes already drawn to Aaron. He's so much taller than I remember. Back in high school, we were more or less the same height, but now he towers over me by at least six inches. Distracted, I find myself staring at the cuts and divots in his abs, the corded muscles of his arms. If I stare any longer, I might drool.

"Aaron!" I yell after standing there for a few more seconds than I'd like. He looks up from filling a row of drinks with ice. "Did I scare you?" I ask, tilting my head, trying to figure out why he's looking at me like that.

He laughs, shaking his head. "No. What's up?"

What's up? Well, for starters, *when did you get so hot?* I keep that internal thought just that. His shaggy, brown hair is tousled just right, and his light brown eyes catch the dim lighting in a way that feels … warm. Inviting.

"Please tell me the guy in the bowling shirt is not buying me drinks," I blurt out, cutting straight to the point.

A smile grows on his face before he says, "It's not him."

"Well, spill already."

Aaron gestures to the wings strapped to his back, pointing to them with both thumbs. "See these wings?" My eyes betray me, scanning his chest and farther down. His abs … *Why am I fantasizing about licking his abs?* "I'm Cupid," he says, and my mind refocuses. "And Cupid doesn't tell."

I groan, throwing my head back for emphasis. "Come on! At least give me a hint."

He hesitates, looking around the room. "Your secret admirer is more obvious than you're thinking."

"Is it the girls?!"

"I gave you a hint." His tone is firmer this time, and for

some reason, it sends a shiver down my spine. *Why did I find that so sexy?* "See these orders? I am working here."

"Fine," I huff, turning on my heel and stomping back to my friends. *So frustrating!*

"You're not messing with me, right?" I ask Emily and Rachel as soon as I reach the table. "These drinks aren't from you guys or from Nicholas being nice?"

"No!" Emily laughs. "Some guy in this bar bought them for you. I'm sure he'll build up the courage soon enough to reveal himself."

"Be patient!" Rachel taps my hand.

I sigh, sinking back into my chair. Patience. *Yeah, right.* This whole secret admirer thing is driving me crazy.

4

Aaron

"Aaron!" Sarah's voice catches me off guard. *Wait, have I been revealed already?* That didn't last long. I haven't even figured out what my next move is yet. There are too many drinks to make and not enough time to think. *Do I get her number? Ask her to dinner?*

"Did I scare you?" she asks, and my eyes quickly check her out. Sarah's always been pretty, but now, this is the most beautiful she's ever been. There's something about her tonight—a confidence, a glow—that makes it hard to focus.

"No," I laugh, taking a deep breath through my nose, trying to keep my composure. "What's up?"

"Please tell me the guy in the bowling shirt is not buying me drinks." She's sassy, impatient, and direct—exactly how I remember her. But there's something about her impatience that draws me in even more. *I can work with that.* I'm going to lean into her curiosity, keep her guessing for as long as I can.

"It's not him," I say coyly, knowing exactly who her secret admirer is.

"Well, spill already."

Absolutely not, I decide right at that moment. I'm not going to reveal my identity until Valentine's Day. I'm going to keep this charade going.

"See these wings?" I gesture with both thumbs, flexing a little more than necessary. Might as well make the most of this ridiculous outfit. "I'm Cupid. And Cupid doesn't tell." I'm already loving this little teasing game.

"Come on! At least give me a hint."

I glance around the room, playing dumb, enjoying the anticipation building between us. "Your secret admirer is more obvious than you're thinking."

"Is it the girls?!" she blurts out, exasperated, and I can't help but laugh. *She has no idea.*

She couldn't be more wrong, and that makes me laugh. My mind races with ideas like sending her little gifts and notes, driving her crazy. I just hope she doesn't have a boyfriend. *Please don't have a boyfriend.* I haven't heard anything around town. I mean, she's at this single's event after all. So I'm hoping that means she's single.

"I gave you a hint," I manage, trying not to let my nerves reveal me. "See these orders? I am working here."

"Fine," she huffs, frustrated but still playful as she turns and walks back to her friends.

Watching her go, all I want is for her to be my Valentine.

5

Sarah

"High Fivers!" the server's voice crackles through the microphone, cutting through the chatter of the bar. "Our God of love, our mixer of drinks, tonight's Cupid, and everyone's favorite—Aaron—is ready for some pics."

"God," I scoff, rolling my eyes at the girls. But even as I say it, my eyes linger on Aaron, and … well, maybe it's not that much of an exaggeration. The more I stare at him, the more that statement feels a little too accurate.

Rachel chuckles, her grin downright mischievous. "It's only fair that I buy you a photo with Aaron."

"No!" I playfully swat her arm. "No. I don't need a photo with Aaron."

"Oh, come on!" Emily protests.

I raise an eyebrow, smirking. "Should I sit on his lap so we can have matching pics?" I tease.

Emily just sticks her tongue out at me. "You're the creative one. Come up with something good."

"Consider it done!"

I scamper over to the photobooth with an extra sway in my step since my secret admirer might be watching.

"Alright, Cherub," I say, standing in front of Aaron. "You strong enough to hold me like I'm a little basket of flowers you're delivering to someone? Let's get my secret admirer riled up."

6

Aaron

I consider for a moment quipping back at Sarah, but instead, I decide to let my actions speak louder than words. Effortlessly, I scoop her up into my arms, lifting her high above my head and to the side, like she's my ballerina in a lift.

The camera flashes. But all too soon, it's over. I set her down gently.

Her eyes rake over me, assessing, before she goes back to her resting sassy face. "That was perfect. Thank you."

Turning away, she goes back to her friends. A little deflated, I reconsider my Valentine's fantasy. Maybe I'll always be Aaron Olson, the barely-one-hundred-pound wrestler she remembers from high school.

The thought pulls me back to senior year, replaying in my mind as I watch her rejoin her friends, laughing.

Just ask her to homecoming. She isn't repulsed by you, you two talk all the time in calculus. You've always had a crush on her, and now it's senior year and you've done nothing about it. Seeing her pull books from her locker, my eyes land on the exposed skin between her low-rise jeans and the hem of her shirt. *She would never say yes.*

"Aaron," she says, and I'm surprised she's talking to me in the halls. I walk toward her, my heart already racing because I want to ask her to homecoming.

"Hey." I smile, seeing the paint stains on her shirt.

"Was it just me, or was the last pop quiz, like, total bullshit?"

"I think he wants us to teach ourselves," I manage while my mind screams to just ask her out.

"Right?! He sucks."

Will you go to homecoming with me? It's a simple question. Just ask her. We hold a growing stare before, "See you in fifth period," comes out of my mouth.

7

Sarah

"Are you fucking kidding me?" Rachel squeals as I get closer to the table. "How is anyone going to top that photo?"

"I hope my secret admirer finds it as interesting," I huff, taking another scan around the room.

"Screw your secret admirer!" Emily pounds the table. Rachel and I both look at her, stunned by her force. "Sarah! Do you not see that shirtless man that just went above and beyond for you and only you?"

"Aaron?" I sigh, looking back over at him doing a simple arm-around-the-shoulder pose with a growing line of women.

"Why not Aaron?" Emily presses, then continues, "He's single. He's classy. Each night at this bar, women are begging to spend one night with him, and he always says no."

"He's too small town."

"And we aren't?" Rachel points at herself and Emily. I bite my lip, considering that. She has a point there. All of the grievances I would have against never leaving your small town would apply to both of them, yet I love them so much. They're my best friends.

"Fine. Do you want me to get his number? I'll do that."

"It's not about what we want. What do you want?" Emily asks.

What a simple yet loaded question that is. *I don't want to be lonely.* I want a guy to snuggle on the couch with. A guy who brings me coffee while I'm consumed by my latest art project. Someone to spend my evenings with. Someone who is passionate about something, who is sure of themself.

What do I really know about Aaron? Nothing that isn't evident right now—that he's a bartender at High Five and shockingly buff.

Fine, I decide internally.

"I'm going to be my own damn Cupid!" I get up from the table and make my way to his line of women. Standing in it, I start to reconsider, but watching him generically pose with woman after woman, I feel more special about the pose we did. *He has to have a little crush on me, right?* Why else would he do that?

"Coming back for seconds?" He raises an eyebrow, and I exhale loudly.

"I have a secret message for Cupid," I whisper, putting my hand next to my lips for effect.

He leans down, and I whisper in his ear, "Roses are red, violets are blue—" His laugh catches me off guard. I almost give up this wild idea but press on. "Give me your number so I can flirt with you."

8

Aaron

Did someone tell her I'm her secret admirer? I'm stunned by her directness and not stupid enough to fumble this opportunity, but I don't want to start a feeding frenzy having all these women in line thinking they can also get my number. I slide my phone out of my back pocket, unlock it, and hand it to her.

"Take this back to your table," I say, low so only she can hear. She grabs it, and I steal the cute sunglasses she's wearing, putting them on. "Add yourself to my contacts. Don't let anyone else see."

"You don't have to be so bossy about it," she sasses, trying to grab her glasses back from me. I playfully grab her wrist, not letting her take them. She squints at me before winking, and I let go. Watching her walk back to her friends, I'm loving that little moment we just shared.

While smiling photo after photo, I'm internally in a state of panic. I still hadn't thought of my next move.

Now what do I do? Ask her on a date? Tell her I was the one who bought her drinks?

"I'm so happy I took tonight off of work," Anna, one of my regulars, says, placing her hand on my chest.

Getting felt up by the local ladies ... it was bound to happen. I wrap an arm around her for the photo, unsure how else to respond. Anna's smiling up at me, and I know she has a crush, but she's barely twenty-two. Too young. I don't want to lead her on.

"The guy in the corner," I say, trying to shift the attention. "He's been checking you out all night."

She glances over. "Not my type." Anna winks before walking away. I barely have time to exhale before another girl slides in for a photo.

Looking back at Sarah, I think sticking to my original plan is best—keep the secret admirer thing going a bit longer. Besides, I want to see what happens when the bar finally calms down. I endlessly replay her little rhyme of "so I can flirt with you." It's too cute. She's always been so creative.

"My phone," I say, approaching her table. Rachel and Emily's eyes widen, and I hope they support this idea of me and Sarah testing the waters.

"Please," she says, sassy as ever. "Please, give me my phone."

I extend my hand. "Please."

"I need these back," she says, grabbing for the heart-shaped glasses.

"No way!" I chuckle, grabbing her hand mid reach, not letting her take them. "Cupid needs these."

She laughs before saying, "Third person, really?"

I shrug, trying to play it cool. Glancing down, I spot a candy heart on the table that reads "UR Cute." *Perfect.* I slide it across the table to her.

She bites her lip, smirking before she sticks her tongue out and puts the candy on it. She teasingly lets it rest there before pulling her tongue back into her mouth.

Fuck. She's serious about flirting with me.

"You have my number now," I manage, turned on and a bit rattled. "It's your move." I wink and walk back to the bar.

9

Sarah

"You better follow up on this," Rachel says with a little arch in her brow.

"Only to get my glasses back," I say, trying to bring my heartrate down from that little moment we just shared.

"Right ... the glasses." Rachel rolls her eyes at me. "Don't get in your head about your 'I'd never date a townie rule' nonsense."

I take a deep breath and another look at Cupid. "One date."

"One date!" Emily cheers.

Looking at my phone, it's nearly 11:00 p.m. "I should go home. I have a Valentine's wreath making class at my studio tomorrow."

Hugging the girls goodbye, I'm more than happy I accomplished both of my goals for the evening: banter and a free drink. *But why didn't my secret admirer reveal himself?*

10

Sarah

Sunday, February 9th

Unlocking the front door of my Main Street Maker's Studio, I'm ready for another day. It's one of those places where you can sign up for a class to make a craft or shop in the store with pre-packed, self-guided kits.

After turning all the lights on and getting out the supplies for my class, I decide to text Aaron. *But what do I even say?*

SARAH ANDERSON

I'm thinking about you.

AARON OLSON

That's flirty.

SARAH ANDERSON

That's what I'm going for. Flirting with you.

I watch the bubbles appear and disappear. They appear again, then disappear. I waste five minutes watching the fucking bubbles until I huff and finish getting ready for my class.

A handful of women begin filling in for the Valentine's wreath event. Helping them get settled, I promptly start the hour-long class. As it progresses, I smile, thinking about how I enjoy teaching and seeing how everyone is creative in their own way. Halfway through, a woman enters, carrying a bouquet of purple flowers.

"For me?" I ask, genuinely surprised.

"Sarah Anderson," she confirms.

"That's you!" one of my regulars booms, excited. "Open the card!"

I open it and laugh. "Tell us!" demands another woman in the class.

"From your secret admirer," I read aloud.

The women swoon.

"To be young again," one of the women says.

"If only my husband would surprise me with gifts," another says.

"So, you don't know who they're from?"

A flurry of questions floods my mind. Is this the same secret admirer from last night? Is the florist already sold out of red and pink flowers? *Purple is my favorite color, though.* These are really pretty flowers. Could they be from Aaron? He left me on read, so I doubt that.

I take a quick picture and send it to Rachel and Emily in our BFF group chat.

SARAH ANDERSON

My secret admirer strikes again.

EMILY BROWN

Pretty flowers!

RACHEL WAGNER

The plot thickens!

Feeling warm and fuzzy, I refocus the group. After everyone is done, I admire the creations as the class cleans up their workspaces.

"Remember, the off season is hard for all of us. Check out my social media for more classes and promos," I say, wrapping up the class.

Once my storefront has cleared out, I check my phone again. Still nothing. I guess I didn't really leave a conversation starter or anything. *It's my move, as he said.*

SARAH ANDERSON

Would you like to get a drink later?

The bubbles immediately appear.

AARON OLSON

On my off days, I prefer not to spend time in a bar.

SARAH ANDERSON

Understandable.

AARON OLSON

When are you free today?

Look at him making a move. Excited, I hope it means he does want to see me today.

SARAH ANDERSON

Well, now. I just finished a class, and the studio has had almost no foot traffic the past couple of weeks. I could close up for the day.

AARON OLSON

Can I come by? I've been meaning to
check it out.

11

Sarah

"This place is so cool!" Aaron says, stepping into the studio. I immediately notice that he is, unfortunately, all bundled up today, wearing a hat and jacket with jeans and boots. He's still all man, looking sexy as ever.

"Thanks." I smile, noticing how the green hat amplifies his light brown eyes while my eyes linger on his amazing bone structure.

"These pieces on the wall. They're yours, right?"

"Yeah," I say, a bit surprised he knows it's my art.

"You have a point of view. I don't know all the fancy art words. But that's clearly a *Sarah Anderson*."

"Too self-promotional?" I ask, although I'm blushing a little.

"Too self-promotional?" he repeats, looking up at me from the watercolor kit he was just examining. "This is your studio. Of course you should have your art for sale." Aaron is taking in the craft kits before saying, "You've always been so talented."

Our eye contact is too intense, and I break away. "This

32

is our bestselling kit." I gesture to the needlepoint pattern of Geneva Lake. "The tourists love it."

He smiles. "Remember that pointillism piece you did of the school mascot? I always thought that was the coolest painting I'd ever seen," Aaron reminisces.

I blush slightly again, my heart fluttering that he remembers that painting. "It was my first commission. So, yeah, this is the space," I say, feeling a little nervous. "I teach classes, sell art kits, and also use it to craft and paint after hours."

"That's great to hear you're still doing art."

I deflect, not knowing how much I should read into Aaron Olson lobbying to be the president of my very small fan club. "My parents are thrilled I'm putting my MFA to work. This is probably one of the best-case scenarios for my degree." I laugh.

"Running a maker's studio? Why downplay it? You're so impressive."

I shrug, loving that he thinks that.

"I'm mad at myself for not coming in sooner," he says, walking toward me. We'd been at a very safe and casual distance before, but now he is standing right in front of me.

"I'm sure you're a bit of a vampire, working at the bar."

He chuckles. "Between the bar and renovating my house, I've been very busy."

"A fellow DIY-er," I say, surprised to learn this little detail.

"I've never really thought about it like that, but yeah. Lots of sweat-equity gutting and rehabbing. You might know the place. It's the old Victorian near the beach."

"The one on the lake?

"Do I look like I have ten million dollars?" He laughs.

"You can never judge a book by its cover. Look at

Nicholas." We both knowingly laugh. "Who would have ever thought Santa had millions in the bank?"

"Or that he'd want to be semi-retired in Lake Geneva," he says, and we both smile.

"Where is your house?" I ask, curious to learn more.

"A block and a half from the public beach, toward the elementary school."

"Oh yeah! That house is going to look so good with some love."

"It was a bit of an impulse purchase. But I think I'll make out whenever I finish it. Hoping to flip it or have it be a summer rental." He tugs the fabric of my coveralls at my hip. "This is so cute."

"You like the paint stains?"

"Yes. Very authentic." My heart rate is telling me that I'm loving this flirting. I'm still reeling with the fact that I'm flirting with Aaron Olson. I need to get over my preconceived notions about him, like him being too "small town" for me. I am back to being a small-town person too, I remind myself.

"The house," he goes back to his earlier conversation. "I thought it would be a one-year project." He laughs. "I'm quickly approaching year two."

"As a fellow property owner, I understand your rehab grievances."

"Oh? Where do you live?"

"Here ... upstairs."

"You own the building?" he asks, shocked.

"It sounds more expensive than it was," I deflect. "My parents helped me with the down payment. It was the money they saved for a wedding. They've lost hope." I chuckle.

"And the mortgage is less than the rent I was paying on the West Coast."

"There's still hope."

"Cupid would know."

"Look at you," he says, leaning on the communal table in the middle of my studio. "Artist, property owner, business owner, town hottie. You're a catch."

Town hottie? I laugh and can't help myself. "Look at you: Cupid by night, carpenter by day, and secret fitness model."

He bites his lip, and fuck does it send a million ideas through my head. "Those are nice," Aaron says, gesturing to the bouquet of flowers on the table.

"Hey!" I yell, maybe too loud. "You never told me who my secret admirer was."

He chuckles, shaking his head slightly. "Valentine's Day is in four days. I think you should let the season run its course."

"I don't like that you know who it is and won't tell me."

"If you weren't so cute when you're frustrated, I might tell you."

12

Aaron

"Have you had lunch?" I ask, loving the banter and energy that's going on between us. She shakes her head. "Would you like to get lunch with me?" As I ask, I wish it would have come out more confident.

"Are you asking me out on a date?" she teasingly asks.

"I know you're the one who's supposed to be flirting with me, but I'm picking up your slack," I tease back in what I hope is a confident smirk.

She giggles, and I'm so attracted to her and all her little mannerisms. She's probably the only person who can make baggy, paint-stained coveralls look this sexy.

"Where do you want to go?" she asks.

"Cakes?"

"Oh! I hope they are still serving their brunch menu."

I take my phone from my pocket, looking at the time. "If we move quickly, we'll make it."

"Let me lock up," she says with almost a skip in her step. Sarah flicks all the lights off, then goes behind the cash register and pulls out a huge puffy coat. In a world where everyone wears black parkas, she opts for a bold, paisley-printed winter coat.

"I like that." I smile.

"Thanks! I love this jacket too!"

As we both step outside, she locks the door behind her. Grabbing her hand, I feel a spark between us, but she pulls away.

"Did I misread this situation?" I ask, needing to understand.

"No."

Nervous, but eager, I flirt, "Am I moving too fast for you?"

She laughs, a devilish glint in her blue eyes. "No."

I take the moment to check her out, making it very clear what my intentions are with her right now. "You're worried your secret admirer might see."

She leans in, her lips dangerously close to mine. "Maybe," she says with a sly smile, then leans back. "But are you trying to get the town in a frenzy? This would be some hot gossip."

I know what she's implying, but I want to hear her say it. "What do you mean?" I ask, grabbing the end of her hair, adding to our flirtation.

"Two staples of Main Street seen walking hand in hand. Juicy stuff," she says in a sexy whisper.

"And you care?" I challenge, my hand grabbing for hers again.

She shoots me a daring look, then squeezes my hand. "No. Let them talk."

I hold back how big my smile wants to be, and we walk toward Cakes.

"When am I getting my glasses back?"

"It wasn't a fair trade? My number for those glasses."

"I didn't agree to a trade. You stole them."

"Stole?"

"Yes, Aaron Olson. You're a petty criminal." She giggles.

We're both smiling so much. I laugh. "Okay. I'll return them." I bite the inside of my cheek, trying to hide how much I'm loving talking with her. "You have little hands," I say as we walk, hand in hand, to the restaurant.

She laughs, and I love how this moment feels right now. So simple and perfect and right. "You just have huge hands," she flirts.

I chuckle, resisting the urge to make any comment about the innuendo. I think about how I could have made a simple move like this in high school to ask her out for a casual meal. I should have done it. But you can't go back. You can only live in the moment. And right now, I'm taking my shot.

It took me far too long to have a normal level of confidence, and today, what I want is Sarah. Her laughter, her warmth, her presence—everything about this feels perfect.

Opening the door for her, we enter Cakes, a local diner known for their huge pancakes and being open twenty-four hours a day.

"Where do you want to sit?"

"A booth."

"Because you're afraid of being in public with me?" I tease.

"Because I don't want half the town talking to us while we're trying to get to know each other," she sasses, then smiles.

I smirk, enjoying this moment. Sitting across from me, she says, "I'm still getting reacclimated to small town living. In Los Angeles, Seattle, and Portland, I was just a girl on the street. Versus here—where I'm Sarah Anderson, daughter of

Bill and Kelly, owner of Main Street Maker's Studio, Class of 2011."

"You lived in Seattle and Portland? I didn't know that."

"You haven't been keeping tabs on me on Facebook?" She arches her brow.

"I'm not on social media anymore."

"Because?" She drags the question out.

"It's so fake."

"Isn't that the truth." She laughs, then looks down at the menu. "My posts used to be very much like 'look at me, living the dream' when really, I was hustling so hard to just get by," she says, not looking up. After a few moments of silence, she says, "I got priced out of all three cities, which is why I'm back here."

"Do you regret it?" I ask, unsure of her tone. "Moving back?"

"Living out west was a great experience to have in my twenties, but living in Wisconsin is easier and calmer. The calm is nice."

"I know what you mean. That's why I like it here too."

"So, have you ever lived anywhere else?"

"Just Lake Geneva, but I travel as much as possible. I love hiking and have been to Argentina and New Zealand, which are some of the best spots for it, and I've also back-packed around Europe a few times."

She makes a little face, like she's almost impressed with me. "I wasn't expecting you to be so worldly."

"Summers at the bar are very good to me. Chicago people are so mad at their money, and I'm happy to rake it in from Memorial Day to Labor Day each year."

"This is my first off season with the studio, and it's hard out there without those damn tourists."

"We should order," I say, pointing to the menu. "Brunch service ends in ten minutes."

"Thanks! Yes."

I wave over the server.

"Eggs Benedict and grapefruit juice for me." Sarah smiles.

"A full stack of pancakes, extra whipped cream."

Sarah laughs, and the server walks away.

"What?"

"Extra whipped cream?"

"I've been eating so clean for the last month. It's cheat day."

A cute noise escapes her.

"What?" I ask, wanting to know.

"Whatever diet and exercise plan you are on, it's working."

I smirk, seeing she's nervous after saying that. Deciding to be bold too, I say, "You know, I've always thought you were cute. Last night's look, though, was really sexy."

"No pants is a good look on me?" she quickly quips.

I laugh, then blush, biting my lip and covering my mouth with my hand, trying to hide the growing innuendos and ideas running through my head.

"Those wings though." She raises a brow. "Those were sexy."

"Just the wings?" I tease, begging her to say more.

"I guess your abs were okay too."

I grab for her hand, swiping my thumb over her knuckles. "I like this look the best," I say, eyeing up her coveralls. "It's so you."

We hold a long stare, our eyes conveying our mutual attraction.

"I always thought you were so cool," I say after a silent moment. "I definitely always noticed you ..."

13

Sarah

We are flirting. I did ask for his number to flirt with him, but I wasn't anticipating us to be flirting so much and so fast.

"I paid attention to you too," I say, then sip my grapefruit juice. "You went to state all four years in wrestling. You're very smart—especially in calculus, but ..." I pause, thinking. "I don't know where you went to college."

"I didn't." He shrugs. "It wasn't for me."

"So, what did you do after high school?"

"A lot of things that affirmed I'm not a career guy. I'm never going to be a career guy."

He takes a bite of his pancakes, and I'm trying not to judge him, but being a forever bartender is not the sexiest thing.

"My version of the American dream ..." he says after finishing a bite, "is rooted in health. Our society doesn't value their health at all." He chuckles to himself. "Hot take, I know. But health is wealth, as they say. That's what I like about the bar. I'm moving around. I'm standing. I'd go crazy if I sat in a chair all day."

"I feel that. I have to be moving around too. It's more for my creative brain, though."

"It's also nice to do something real, something tangible rather than stare at a screen and live more in a digital world than the real one."

I smile, deleting the judgment I'd just passed on him. He knows who he is, and he knows what he wants. That's sexy. "We have so much in common." I smile.

"That we're both good with our hands?"

"Very risqué for brunch, Aaron," I whisper with a growing blush on my cheeks.

He chuckles, and it's sending me. Our chemistry. It's there.

As we finish our meal, I note that he ate every single bite on his plate.

"Nicholas and I had a little competition going for last night," he says, picking up on me staring at his plate.

"Oh?"

"Sorry to disappoint. I'm not usually that leaned out. I barely touched carbs the past month. We were both cutting."

"You two definitely took the competition seriously," I manage, trying everything I can to not think about him shirtless.

"I take everything I do seriously," he says, fucking dangerously.

Our server drops the check on the table, and he grabs it. I'm still reeling from all of this flirtation.

"Cash?" I say, surprised he didn't plop down a credit card and instead counts out the perfect amount with a generous tip.

"For small businesses, I always pay in cash. You should get that."

"Losing three percent on each transaction definitely adds up." I smile at how he's thoughtful and considerate. "Thanks for brunch."

"You're a great date." He smiles. "Let me walk you back."

"Such a gentleman," I quip while standing from the booth.

He grabs my hand, this time interlacing his fingers with mine. He's holding my hand with more confidence than before. As we walk, we look at each other, exchanging little smiles. *Am I going to invite him up?* I want to, but I also don't want to rush this.

"I really enjoyed that," Aaron says as we approach my studio.

"Me too." I smile, staring up at him.

We stand there, holding hands, our eyes glued to each other. My lips signal exactly what I'm thinking as they part, begging for him to kiss me.

"You're so beautiful," he says, gently pulling me toward him.

I'm going to do it—kiss Aaron Olson.

His full lips press into mine at that perfect pressure, the one that makes you want to slide your tongue right in, the one that makes you want to keep going and never stop. It's been too long since I've kissed anyone, longer still since I've felt this way from a kiss. It's perfect, until he pulls away.

"Aaron Olson," I breathe, nearly commanding him to come back.

"Sarah Anderson," he growls. "Let me take you out for dinner."

"When?"

"Tomorrow."

"Tomorrow?"

"Sunday and Monday are my weekends," he shares.

"Where are we going?" I ask, smiling and wanting to kiss him again.

"La Nonna."

"Fancy."

"You're fancy."

"You're right." I smile

"7:00 p.m.," he breathes, leaning back into me.

I wrap both hands around his neck, feeling the heat between us intensify. This time, I want to kiss him for far longer than the first go around. His lips meet mine again, and I lose myself in the sensation, feeling weak in the knees. My heart rate soars as he squeezes my waist, pulling me into his hard body. I taste the sweet syrup on his tongue and consciously hold back from mauling him, not letting my touch escalate this scene past a great make out on Main Street.

"7:00 p.m.," I softly say, pulling away.

He leans right back in, placing a baby kiss on my lips, then smiles.

"Now I know why you won't tell me who my secret admirer is."

"Why's that?" He tilts his head, his smile still glued on his face.

"You don't want the competition."

"Something like that," he says with a smolder in his eyes that makes me want to rip his jacket and shirt right off. *But we can wait.* Watching him walk away, my heart is racing with excitement, and I text the BFF group chat.

SARAH ANDERSON

I just kissed Aaron Olson …

RACHEL WAGNER

What?!

EMILY BROWN

Details! Now!

SARAH ANDERSON

He came to the studio, asked me to lunch
… and we made out in front of my studio.

EMILY BROWN

And?

SARAH ANDERSON

And it was good enough for me to agree to
a second date. It's tomorrow at La Nonna.

RACHEL WAGNER

OOO! He likes you!

EMILY BROWN

Tres fancy!

14

Aaron

I *just kissed Sarah Anderson.* Walking fast with my hands in my pockets, I'm unsure what to do with all of this nervous, excited energy. Replaying our kisses, I love how her big, blue eyes looked up at me, the way she wrapped her arms around my neck, demanding more.

Back at my house, I decide to text her.

AARON OLSON

Still thinking about our kiss.

SARAH ANDERSON

Me too.

What should my next secret admirer surprise be? Should I reveal myself at dinner tomorrow? I've come this far; I want to play it out more. But I have to work the rest of the week. Valentine's Day is on Friday. How am I going to give her the best Valentine's Day when I have to work on Friday?

15

Sarah

Monday, February 10th

S taring at my closet, I have no idea what to wear and text the BFF group chat.

I try on so many outfits and send them photos of my three favorites. One is a long-sleeved dress with tights and heeled boots that hit at the knee. Another is a flowy top and wide-leg black jeans, and the last outfit is a plunging long-sleeved bodysuit and wide-leg dark jeans.

RACHEL WAGNER

Last option!

EMILY BROWN

Agree!

I stare at myself in the mirror. This is a flirty look for a flirty date, and I'm really excited to see him again. It's the third day in a row.

AARON OLSON

I'm about to walk past your place. Meet me out front?

SARAH ANDERSON

You're walking? It's freezing out.

AARON OLSON

I live less than a half mile from La Nonna. It would be silly to drive. You coming down?

SARAH ANDERSON

Yes.

I toss on my coat and skip the hat, not wanting to mess up my hair. La Nonna isn't even two blocks from here. Walking down the stairs, I exit out the front, and Aaron's there in his puffy coat and hat.

"Hi," he breathes, grabbing my hand and pulling me in for a kiss. It catches me off guard in a good way.

As the gentle kiss comes to a natural stopping point, I really stare into his light brown eyes and find them so intriguing.

"Hi." I smile up at him. It was bold for him to greet me with a kiss. I liked it ... a lot.

He interlaces his gloved fingers with mine, and we walk to La Nonna, the fanciest restaurant in Lake Geneva. Aaron opens the door for me, I smile, and the hostess takes us to a booth. Sliding my coat off, I catch Aaron's voice—barely a whisper—saying, "Whoa."

I shoot him a challenging look, though I can't help but feel flattered by his reaction.

"You look incredible," he says, his eyes locked with mine before quickly darting down. "I mean, you're always stylish, but—wow."

I want to swoon, but instead, I sass, deflecting the praise. "Am I making you nervous?"

He leans in slightly, his voice low and intense. "You're giving me a lot of ideas."

For once, I don't have anything to say. I bite my lip, also having some ideas, and take my seat at the booth.

"You don't look half bad," I tease, checking out his thick cowl neck sweater that I want to snuggle into.

"Well, what a nice surprise to see you in here for once," our server in her early twenties says, approaching our table. She's smiling so much at Aaron. It's a nice distraction from staring at him and fantasizing about all the trouble we could get into after dinner.

"Hey, Anna." Aaron smiles. "This is Sarah."

"You own the Maker's Studio, right?" she asks.

"That's me," I quip with a smile, noticing how she is lusting after Aaron. I mean, I get it, girl. I definitely get it.

"What would you like to drink?" She looks at me.

"Um, I need a minute." I haven't even looked at the menu. Aaron and I have essentially been eye fucking each other since we sat down.

"Let me guess, Aaron," Anna says, moving her gaze back to him. "You'll have a gin and tonic?"

"Not tonight," he lightly says. "We're going to have a bottle of your house red."

"Great." She smiles at him, so friendly and eager. "And I'll drop by High Five sometime this week."

I chuckle as she walks away.

"What?" Aaron asks.

"You can be so bossy. What if I didn't like red wine?"

"You like it," he softly says, tilting his brow and resuming his heated stare with me.

"And she's very friendly with you." I laugh, sweating at the intensity of this date so far. I take a sip of my water, trying to cool down.

"I'm a local bartender. It's part of the job."

"Flirting with all your patrons?"

"Sometimes." Aaron laughs. I like that rich, hearty sound too much. I'm liking everything about him too much.

"So, am I just another patron?"

"I don't recall you paying for a single drink." He grabs my hand. "Not much of a patron if you aren't paying, no?"

I softly chuckle. *He's witty.* I like that.

Bringing us a decanter full of wine and two glasses, Anna's eyes are locked on his hand, playing with my fingers. She's clearly shocked and walks away.

"Did you sleep with her and never call her back or something?" I joke.

"No. Definitely not. She just comes into the bar after work a lot."

"Emily said something about there being a line out the door of girls trying to get with you."

"And?"

"You're really making me work for your answers here." I squint at him.

"I told you: When you're frustrated, you're cute. But ... yeah, I never date locals. You should feel special that I'm breaking my little rule for you."

"That's my rule!" I nearly yell. "I don't date locals."

"Looks like we've broken our rule twice now."

We hold a heated stare.

"You must've had at least a one-night stand with someone from the bar," I press.

"Never."

"Never?" I test.

"I'm more of a let's wait until the third date kind of guy versus a one-night guy."

"Full of surprises," I muse, a little deflated that it won't be happening tonight. But if we go out on another date … it could happen. Oh, how I would love for that to happen—to lick his abs and get lost in the sheets with him.

16

Aaron

"I'm going to order the osso buco. Get whatever you want." I admire Sarah as she reads and re-reads the menu. As much as I love her legs, this top is too damn sexy. Her chest is right on the edge of a wardrobe malfunction. It's taking so much willpower to keep my eyes off her perfect, definitely more-than-a-handful-sized tits.

"There are too many options," Sarah says, stress in her tone.

"Have you ever had their homemade pasta? It's great."

She shields her lips with her hand, whispering, "I've actually never been here before."

"You haven't supported a fellow Main Street business?" I tease and am honestly surprised this is her first time being here.

"I know ... I'm on a pretty tight budget with the studio and the building's mortgage right now. Fine dining isn't exactly something I'm allocating for at the moment."

I grab my glass, raising it up for a toast. "To splurging on special occasions and supporting our Main Street businesses. And to financial responsibility—because it's incredibly sexy."

She giggles, and I mean it. She is so dynamic and independent, and that is very sexy.

"For your paintings, what's your style?" I ask, trying to keep the conversation light, but also wanting to know more about her.

"I'm a mood painter," she admits with a slight smile. "Probably why I've had a hard time establishing a brand. I just want to paint what I feel like, when I feel like it, in whatever style matches my mood."

Before I can respond, Anna arrives at the table. "A little gift from our kitchen," she says, sliding us a dish of arancini. "Do you both know what you'd like to order?"

I look at Sarah, and she nods, saying, "I'll have the homemade pasta with mussels."

"Great choice. And you, Aaron?"

"Osso buco."

"You'll love that," she purrs, staring deep into my eyes. "Since when did you two start dating?"

Sarah chuckles, and I know that whatever I say is going to be used in a game of telephone throughout the town. "It's new." I smile at Sarah, grabbing her hand again.

"Just in time for Valentine's Day. How cute," Anna says in a tone that could be taken as sarcastic before walking away.

"It's new," Sarah repeats, her face beaming.

I wish I could have told Anna that she's my girlfriend. Now there's something I haven't thought or wished for in a long time. But I want it. I want Sarah to be my girlfriend.

"So, what are you up to this weekend?" I change the subject, not ready to admit how easy the connection is with Sarah and how comfortable I feel with her already.

"I'm teaching a kids' watercolor class on Saturday in the late afternoon and a needlepoint class on Sunday morning. Otherwise, I'll be fiddling around in the studio hoping some people come in to buy some kits or want to craft. What about you?"

"I'm working on figuring out how I'm going to see you again."

"Swoon," she teases. "I could always stop by the bar on Saturday and make your fan club jealous."

"Fan club?" I groan at the insinuation.

"Wait!" she says, too excited. "Are you wearing your wings on Friday? I might have to come by if you are."

"I think the wings were a one-night-only special." I take a sip of my wine, considering if I should just say it—tell her I'm her secret admirer. But I like the growing idea of coming up with one more special surprise as part of the reveal.

"You should really wear them on Friday. It's Valentine's Day!"

"We'll have to see. How about you plan on not making plans on Friday evening, and we can go from there?"

"Sounds like not a plan." She winks. "So, what were you up to today, before dinner?"

"Woodworking."

She giggles mid sip, and I shake my head with a smile. "Get your head out of the gutter. I'm building a new banister for the house."

"I'd love to see your place."

"Yeah?" *She wants to see my place?* Should I read into it? I want to read into it.

"For the woodworking. I'd like to see your attention to detail," Sarah flirts.

Shaking my head again, with a smirk glued on my face, I

refill her glass. "I'm only biting my tongue because we're in public," I say and take a moment to check her out again.

This date is going incredibly well, and I can't help but think about what comes next. It's only our second date, and I have a rule about not taking anyone back this soon. But being with Sarah feels different. The chemistry between us is undeniable, and I'm more than tempted to show her my place.

"What about you?" I refocus on the present, staring at Sarah. "What were you up to today?"

"I spent too much time putting this outfit together."

"Sarah Anderson, nervous. That's a cute mental image."

She furrows her brows, disagreeing with me. "So, when did you get this tall?" she asks. "I don't remember you being this tall in high school."

"When I was twenty." I pause, taking a sip of my wine. "I know it's weird. But that's when I stopped growing."

She chuckles a little.

"You're fucking naughty," I whisper, and she blushes a little.

"When did you get buff?" she asks, eyeing me.

"Over the last few years. I really enjoy calisthenics with a little weightlifting."

"Just a little weightlifting?" she asks flirtatiously.

"Enough that I can throw you around sometime."

"You think that's what I want?" she asks in a high-pitched, maybe nervous, tone.

I take the opportunity to slowly rake my eyes down her, savoring everything about this flirtation and the way she looks. "I know that's what you want."

17

Sarah

"Pasta with mussels." Anna slides the dish in front of me, interrupting the fucking intensity of our flirting. "Osso buco, for you." She smiles at Aaron. This time around, however, he doesn't even look at her. I have his full attention, and it's intoxicating.

"More wine?" Anna asks.

"Up to you." Aaron smiles.

I'm in no rush for this date to end.

"Why not?"

Our server clears the empty decanter and appetizer dishes, and Aaron grabs my hand, spinning his thumb around each of my fingers one by one.

"You are such a flirt," I say once we're alone again.

"Me?" he responds, feigning innocence, taking a bite of his food. His eyes are revealing him, and the charged air between us is only thickening. "Your top ... you are the flirt."

"It's a bodysuit," I correct.

He leans in closer, "It's fucking hot."

My cheeks flush. "Not as hot as the wings," I say, spinning the pasta onto my fork.

"Hmm," he hums with a wink, making me laugh again. "So," Aaron begins, "what's something you've always wanted to do but haven't had the chance to yet?"

"In bed?" I tease. "But for real ... dining here. Seriously, thank you. I've always wanted to check it out."

"Eh niente," he says.

"So cultured," I tease, waiting for him to tell me what that means.

"It's nothing—in Italian."

"I think tonight is much more than nothing."

My tone is more honest and revealing than I'd like to let on, but it's definitely true. All of the time I've spent with Aaron the last couple of days is anything but nothing. It's everything. I take a sip of my wine, considering how I'm falling for Aaron Olson.

"What about you? What's something you've wanted to do that you haven't had the chance to yet?"

"Sarah Anderson," he says before taking a sip of his wine.

I huff a laugh, dying at how we are on the same page. He's blushing after saying that, and I guess the third glass of wine for each of us is making things very interesting. Yet, he's the one that says we have to wait until the third date.

"Did you two save any room for dessert?" Anna asks, and it nearly startles me. Aaron and I have been so deep in this little love bubble that I didn't even notice her approach.

"Just the check," Aaron says.

"So bossy," I manage, flustered by how hot I am finding every little thing about him. "What if I wanted dessert?"

"When did I say you weren't getting it?"

I'm too nervous to ask what that means, hoping it's something dirty.

Anna slides the check on the table, and Aaron reaches for his wallet.

"How much cash do you carry around?" I ask, truly shocked at how thick the bills portion of his wallet is.

"Enough."

"I guess I'm still paranoid about someone robbing me," I share. "Living in cities makes you cautious." *But of course, that would never happen here, someone stealing your wallet.*

"Ready?" he asks, and I nod. He grabs my jacket, helping me put it on.

"Such a gentleman."

"For now," he whispers in my ear.

Fuck. Is this going to happen?

18

Aaron

Holding Sarah's hand as we walk from La Nonna to her studio, I only have a couple of minutes to make up my mind. Well, maybe less with how fast we are walking in the cold. *Am I going to sleep with her? Or am I going to wait?* I think she would say yes if it came up. I hope she would, but I can't rush this. I shouldn't rush this. I don't want to rush this.

Standing outside her dark storefront, I lift up our interlaced hands, kissing the back of hers, noticing how cold it is.

"Do you want to come up?" Sarah asks, shivering.

"Of course—but not tonight."

She moans a disappointed sound, and it's the cutest thing I've ever heard.

"Counter offer," she says, her teeth chattering. "Hot make out in my stairwell right now."

"Lead the way." I laugh.

She takes the ring of keys from her jacket pocket and turns toward the door. I stand behind, placing my hands on her hips before kissing her neck.

"Stop distracting me. It's fucking freezing out here."

"No."

She giggles, unlocking the door and pushing it open.

My heart rate immediately increases as we step inside, and I decide to go for it, to make this make out hot and wild and a preview of what our next date could be like. Pushing her against the wall, I grumble, "You want to see bossy? Unzip your jacket for me."

She wets her lips, holding the metal zipper, teasing me, not pulling it down.

"Unzip your jacket," I command, staring at her. The stairwell is cold, but not below freezing like outside. It will be worth it for what I have in mind.

"Okay," she breathes with a growing smile on her face. Slowly pulling the zipper down, she's teasing me. Her eyes are taunting me.

"Good girl," I praise, holding her gaze. Sarah's face goes red, and she sticks out her tongue biting it. *Exactly.* I knew it. "Sassy girls always want someone to boss them around," I breathe, kissing her newly exposed cleavage.

"Maybe," she says, her breath catching as I trail my tongue from her chest to her neck.

"Definitely."

Digging my hand into the back of her head, I pull her hair slightly and kiss her neck. Placing my hand on her chest, she immediately squirms. *My hand is cold.* Pressing her firmly against the wall, I kiss up to her chin, then place small kiss after small kiss along her jaw.

"Stop teasing me," Sarah whines, wrapping her arms around my neck.

"Why?"

She huffs, and I grab her face, slamming my lips into hers. Sarah pulls me in closer. Her lips. Her taste. Her smell. I'm consumed by her. My hands have a mind of their own, trailing down her body as we keep kissing. Squeezing her hips, I close the distance between our bodies. Sliding my hand down the fabric of her jeans, I squeeze her thigh, then pick her leg up, wrapping it around my hip. Our kisses are escalating. They're becoming demanding, heated.

I'm hard and seriously reconsidering going upstairs with her. *I want it.* I want it so fucking bad.

With one hand squeezing her thigh, the other is teasingly exploring her cleavage before sliding under the fabric of her bodysuit. She flinches at the touch.

"Sorry," I breathe, knowing how cold my fingers are.

"Copping a feel, huh?" she says with a light laugh.

I open my eyes and see the sex blazing in hers. On an impulse, I trail my tongue down her neck and flick it around her nipple while I hold her breast. *Her tits are amazing.* I can't believe she was braless all night.

"Mmm," she moans, and her hand rubs me over my pants. "Um," she breathes, "has anyone told you that you're an amazing kisser?"

"Has anyone told you how sexy you are?" I squeeze her ass with both hands, lifting her off the ground.

"Let's go upstairs," she whispers.

"Next time," I breathe, putting her back down. "I should go." The ache is evident in my voice.

"You're going to leave me like this?"

"Like what?" I tease, knowing what she means.

"Fucking hot and bothered."

"Yes," I say, staring into her hungry blue eyes.

"Second base, seriously?"

"I will more than make up for it next time."

"Aaron," she pleads, and I almost give in.

"I promise," I say, pulling her in for a goodnight kiss.

The kiss lingers, and I love how sweet it is. "May I leave?" I ask as she doesn't move from the door.

She huffs.

"Frustrated. It's too damn cute." I kiss her again. "Goodnight, Sarah."

"Goodnight, Aaron."

19

Sarah

Hot, bothered, and a little drunk, I walk up the stairs to the second-floor apartment I live in. My phone buzzes, and I take it out of my jacket pocket.

Oh, really?

He's having too much fun making me frustrated. He needs to be more frustrated. I throw my jacket to the floor and unbutton my pants, which are so snug after that meal. As I walk to my bedroom, a wicked idea comes to mind. Taking out my vibrator from my nightstand, I snap a picture of me kissing it and text it to Aaron.

20

Aaron

"Fuck," I breathe, seeing this photo of Sarah. *I need to take Friday night off of work.* I'm more than half tempted to go back to her place. I guess I fumbled the dessert bit. I'll make it up to her, though.

Tapping Nicholas's name in my contacts, I know it's late.

"How much would you hate me if I took Friday off?" I ask as he answers.

"You're the manager. You don't have to ask me." He chuckles. "Why do you need the night off?"

"Sarah—"

He interrupts, saying, "Approved," with a knowing laugh.

"Approved?"

"Emily would kill me if I prevented Sarah from finding out who her secret admirer is."

"How do you know about that?"

"She made a comment to me yesterday, and it clicked—since you are the one that comped the shots and a custom cocktail for their table."

"Thanks, man. I know Friday is going to be busy."

"Obviously, you have to find some people to pick up your shift. We should really start recruiting for the seasonal hires too ... so we can take our time off now before we're really slammed this summer."

He hangs up, and I take a deep breath, staring at the photo again. *Friday.* It's only four days. I'm beyond tempted to go back to her place right now. Friday is Valentine's Day. It's perfect to wait.

Looking at the time, I decide to cash in one more favor with the owner of the local bakery. It's time to reveal myself as Sarah's secret admirer and give her the best Valentine's Day ever.

21

Sarah

Tuesday, February 11th

A woman walks into the studio minutes after I open with a present in hand.

"For you," she says.

Surprised, I open the box and find a purple, heart-shaped cookie and a small card. In white icing, the cookie says, "Will you be my Valentine?" I smile, hoping it's from Aaron, and open the card.

ROSES ARE RED, VIOLETS ARE BLUE, I'D LIKE TO
COOK DINNER FOR YOU
— YOUR SECRET ADMIRER,
AARON OLSON

I laugh, beaming with delight. *Aaron?!* Why didn't he just tell me?! He's too cute. *Purple.* My drink was purple, the flowers were purple, this cookie is purple. How does he know my favorite color? Were my friends helping him?

I open up my text thread with Aaron and begin typing.

SARAH ANDERSON

Of course I'll be your Valentine! Thank you
for the belated dessert too.

AARON OLSON

Are you surprised?

SARAH ANDERSON

More than I should be! I guess it was
obvious.

How do you know that my favorite color is
purple?

AARON OLSON

Who could forget when you wore nothing
but purple to school for a month?

I grimace, thinking about how I've always been a little bit of an odd duck.

SARAH ANDERSON

I was expecting some kind of response
after that picture I sent last night …

AARON OLSON

I couldn't think of anything respectful
to say.

"You don't have to be respectful," I mumble, happy my studio is empty right now. "Shit!" He's calling me.

"Good morning, Valentine," I purr, or at least try my best to sound sexy.

"Friday. Come over to see my woodworking and cooking skills."

I giggle. "Don't you have to work?"

"Not anymore."

"What time?"

"7:00 p.m."

"It's a date."

"The third date," he growls, then hangs up the phone.

I'm going to fuck Aaron Olson. I giggle, then bite my lip, thinking about my buff cherub.

Opening up the BFF group chat, I text the girls.

SARAH ANDERSON

My secret admirer has revealed himself …

RACHEL WAGNER

Oh?!

SARAH ANDERSON

It's Aaron Olson!

EMILY BROWN

Of course it's Cupid!

SARAH ANDERSON

This Friday will be our third date …

RACHEL WAGNER

Get it, girl!!

EMILY BROWN

Valentine's Day! You better have fun with that.

22

Aaron

Wednesday, February 12th

Zoning off at the bar, I think about menu idea after menu idea for Friday. Slow cooked duck breast? Lobster ravioli?

"Aaron!" I look across the bar and see Anna smiling at me, breaking my thoughts.

"Hey, what can I get you?"

"Surprise me," she says, and the flirty tone catches me off guard. "I thought you didn't hook up with anyone within a ten-mile radius of here?" Anna asks while I mix together a new cocktail recipe I'm playing with.

"I don't. Well, I didn't."

She pouts, and I don't quite know how to respond.

Placing the drink in front of her, I manage, "Enjoy."

"Tell me what's in it." Anna grabs my hand. I know she's always had a crush on me, but this outright flirtation is stronger than past visits. I begin to pull away, but she squeezes my hand tighter. Emily walks in the door, her eyes darting to Anna's hand on top of mine. "Fuck," I softly mutter.

Emily furrows her brows as she walks closer to the bar.

"Anna," I scold, pulling my hand back again. "Emily," I greet. "How are you?"

"Good," she says, tight.

Bar social dynamics begin whirling through my mind. Women flirt with me, and I, historically, have always given them a little flirt back. It's part of being a bartender, after all.

"What can I get you?" I ask Emily.

"I'm good. Waiting for Nicholas." Her tone remains tight.

Emily's tone is telling me that she thinks there is more to what she just walked in on. I can't start a whole scene right now by publicly dissing Anna in front of everyone.

"He's in the office. Let me take you there," I suggest, hoping to get a few seconds alone with Emily to explain.

"Sure," she says, picking up what I'm putting down.

I meet her at the end of the bar, and we walk toward the back of the place.

"It's not what it looked like."

"Says every innocent man."

She's a good friend for thinking that. *Fuck*. I remember now that her ex cheated on her in one of those *everyone knew around town before she did* kind of ways. I understand why she's having a heightened reaction to what she saw.

"You know I give the ladies a little flirt, but Anna grabbed my hand right as you walked in. I had no intention of reciprocating that. I'm so into Sarah."

"Are you?"

"She's all I think about. Before Anna grabbed my hand,

I was planning our dinner menu on Friday. I can't wait to see her again."

"People talk," Emily says, the chill in her tone thawing. "I don't want Sarah to think there is something going on with anyone that comes into the bar. She's going to hear things."

Now that I'm dating Sarah, we're going to have to talk about bar dynamics. She's going to have to be secure in the fact that I'm never going to cross the line, like give my number to someone else or meet up outside of the bar.

"I know."

"Please don't fuck this up, Aaron."

I smile. "So, you like the idea of me and Sarah?"

"Yes."

I point over my shoulder, happy to hear her approval. "I should get back to the bar."

Emily's blessing keeps a smile glued to my face as I head back. I *really* like the idea of Sarah and me too.

23

Sarah

Friday, February 14th

Since you're handling dinner, I'll bring dessert.

What kind of dessert are we talking about?

That depends.

On?

Your tastes.

I'm not picky.

Chocolate covered strawberries and a surprise.

AARON OLSON

I like surprises.

SARAH ANDERSON

Aaron Olson …

AARON OLSON

Sarah Anderson.

SARAH ANDERSON

I'm sweating.

AARON OLSON

Not as much as you will be after dinner.

I bite my lip, loving this flirtation, and decide to leave him on read for a change. "I don't have anything respectful to say." I giggle to myself.

24

Aaron

Looking up from my phone, my cheeks are flushed. Thank God I made a grocery list for once. All my brain can think about right now is Sarah. I look down at my list, then back at the produce section, grabbing spinach and arugula. Maybe I should add some cherry tomatoes? Another crunchy item would be a good idea. Walnuts or pecans? Yeah, let's go with walnuts. She's definitely going to make a quip about nuts. I smile, looking forward to seeing her and thinking about her sass.

Pushing my cart to the butcher offerings, the filet mignon looks perfect. *Wine.* I definitely need a good bottle of red wine to pair with the steak. Something bold like a Cabernet Sauvignon or a Merlot.

I look at the labels. I should get a funny one, one she can make a comment about. Not seeing anything that looks good with a funny name, I go with something nice instead. Something that says I'm very serious about treating my Valentine. At just under one hundred dollars, Caymus Cabernet Sauvignon it is.

Holding the bottle of wine in my hands, I wonder—

should I ask her to be my girlfriend? Since we've started talking, it's been so natural. I've loved every second.

Flowers! I almost forgot flowers for the table and for her to take home. Red roses? No. That's not her. *Oh!* They have purple roses, perfect. I make a nice bouquet with the roses and lavender stock.

Walking toward the checkout, I spot one of my regulars, Karen. *Agh,* I internally groan, not wanting to make idle chit chat.

"Someone is one lucky lady!" Karen smiles, eyeing my cart.

I smile politely.

"Please, tell me! Who finally got Aaron Olson's attention?"

"Sarah Anderson."

"The artist! How cute! Oh my God, you two would have the most beautiful babies."

I laugh, not disagreeing.

"Oh, and it's Valentine's Day!" She swoons. "I won't keep you. It looks like you have a lot to do."

"Happy Valentine's Day, Karen." I smile and start pushing my cart to the checkout. "Oh!" I mutter to myself. I should get candles. I bite my lip, thinking about later. I should get some more condoms too.

25

Sarah

Dipping the strawberries in melted chocolate, I'm full-on fantasizing about tonight. He's going to need to pull those wings out of retirement. *Those fucking wings*. I bite my lip.

After dipping the last strawberry, I place it on the serving tray to rest with the others and lick the chocolate off the spoon. On a flirty whim, I send Aaron a picture of me licking the spoon. Aaron's response is immediate.

AARON OLSON

I have nothing respectful to say.

I laugh, walking to the shower to get ready for tonight.

Wrapped in a towel, I stare at my underwear drawer. I put on a matching pink lace bra and underwear set, leaning into the Valentine's Day theme. Aaron's hands touching me, like how he did after our last date, play and replay in my memory. Grabbing a condom from my nightstand, I slide it into one of the cups of my bra. Smiling, I think that will be a fun surprise for later.

My surprise! I almost forgot about the whipped cream I bought. I can't forget that.

My secret admirer really seemed to be into my legs at the bar. Going through my closet, I decide on a red, long-sleeved, v-neck sweater dress. I typically wear tights with it since it's so short, but tonight ... I'll skip those. Looking at my shoes, it would be a bit much to wear heels, so I decide instead to wear over-the-knee, tan, suede boots.

Giving myself one final look in the mirror, I think I look very fuckable and hope it happens.

While Aaron doesn't mind walking a half mile in the cold, I do. I put the whipped cream in my bag and carry the chocolate covered strawberries to my car.

26

Aaron

The doorbell rings, and my nerves take over. Looking at my phone, I'm stressed since the meal isn't where I had hoped it would be right now. So prompt, I chuckle to myself, seeing that it's exactly 7:00 p.m. I'm so excited to see Sarah this evening.

I turn down the burners, then make my way to the front of the house to greet her.

"Wow," I breathe, opening the door, seeing inches of leg exposed, not covered by her coat or boots.

"I was half expecting you to be wearing the angel wings." She smiles, and I take the tray of chocolate covered strawberries from her, ushering her inside.

"They already did their magic," I say, closing the door and keeping the freezing wind from entering any longer.

"Oh, yeah?"

"Well, you're here ... on Valentine's Day."

"What am I going to do with my corny cherub?" She laughs, leaning into me for a kiss. "Slippers? I never would have guessed you were a slippers guy," she says, looking at my feet.

"This old house … it's drafty. My feet are always cold."

Taking her jacket off, she hangs it on the coat rack and then starts unzipping her boots.

"No." I stop her. "Leave those boots on. I love them … and you don't want cold feet."

Sarah winks at me, and I bite my tongue. *We have to eat dinner first.* She is mesmerizing in the shortest red dress and over-the-knee boots … "You look great."

"You don't look so bad yourself," she says, pulling at my fitted, maroon, knit sweater. "Is this the banister?" she asks, looking at the stairs.

"Yes."

"Such a good woodworker," she teases, running her hands up and down it. "Now, give me a tour."

Shaking my head, I hold back a lot of funny comebacks. "Well, this is the entry way, take a right … into the dining room," I say, guiding us.

"I have to put something in your fridge too. It's a surprise," she says, holding her bag. "Candles!" she cheers, seeing the array of candles on the dining room table and around the fireplace. "You are such a romantic."

"I try."

"These smells!" she moans as we walk into the kitchen. It's every kind of indication of what she will be sounding like later. I bite the inside of my cheek, not revealing how hot I found that noise.

After examining the pans on the stovetop, she says, "This house is so nice! You did all of it yourself?"

"Don't be so surprised," I tease, and she flashes me a sassy little look. "The floors, tile, paint, refinishing the hard-wood … all me."

"Very impressive. Now don't look, I'm putting some-thing in your fridge."

She twirls her finger, signaling me to turn around. I turn away from her, curious what this surprise could be.

"Okay. You can turn around again." She giggles mischievously.

"Can I pour you a glass of wine?" I ask, stepping closer to her.

"Please."

"Good girl," I tease. "Being so polite."

She swats my chest, but the new pink on her cheeks tells me she loved that.

"The bottle has been decanting for about an hour. It should be perfect," I share, pouring her a glass, then myself one. "Happy Valentine's Day," I cheers her, staring into her beautiful blue eyes while we each take a sip.

"What is this?" she asks after taking her first sip, her eyes lighting up.

"Something special. Dinner's almost ready. Give me a couple of minutes to finish up. Go relax in the dining room."

"So bossy," she whispers with a smirk. "I can help."

"That's okay, Legs. I want to spoil you."

"How can I say no to that?" She leans into me, kissing me. Watching her walk away, I take another sip of my wine. "Legs," I muse to myself, staring at hers, then refocus on plating dinner.

27

Sarah

Taking a few deep breaths while alone in the dining room, I can't believe how much effort he put into tonight's dinner. Sipping this amazing wine, I feel so special. Looking around the Victorian home's dining room, all of the little details pop out at me. He hasn't cut any corners in his renovation or this dinner date. *I love this home.* It's definitely not a bachelor pad. It's elegant, inviting, and warm.

He emerges from the kitchen, his hands holding appetizer plates.

"Do you really not believe that you're creative?" I ask, as he sets a beautifully plated salad in front of me.

"I'm not." He chuckles.

"Tell that to this dish ... and your house."

He shrugs, then says, "I can't paint like you. That's for sure."

"Creativity comes in many forms."

He sits across the table from me, and we take our first bites of the salad.

"I've never considered that I was artsy or creative," he says, like he's been ruminating on my comment.

"You are very creative, Aaron Olson!"

The face he makes ... he's still unsure about it. That's so crazy.

"Tell me more about your studio," he says, grabbing for my hand across the table. "When did it officially open?"

"Officially in April, but I bought the building last February."

"Time flies, right? I had no idea you've been back in town for a year."

"It was a whirlwind ... buying the building and turning the ground-floor retail into Main Street Maker's Studio."

"You're kicking ass!"

"I'm getting by." I sigh.

"Most businesses fail in the first year. I think you're doing great."

"I haven't really made it a year yet," I deflect.

"Plan on closing before April?"

"No."

He laughs, and I agree. I should be prouder of myself and my business. "The first off season was tough though. Lots of key learnings for next year."

"Like?"

"Maybe some virtual classes and an e-store so people can have kits shipped to their house."

"Love those ideas." He takes a sip of his wine.

"When is your next big trip?" I ask, curious to know more about him.

"I don't know yet. I'm hoping to get one in before the summer rush, but I really want to finish up this house."

"You've put so much work in. Are you sure you want to part with it once you're done renovating?"

"I'm a single guy. If I lived in a small apartment, it would give me so much more cash to live life with."

"What if you weren't a single guy?" I can't believe I said it after it came out. Flustered, I sip my wine, gathering myself.

"Maybe I would have a different opinion. This house would be great for a family."

We both look down at our salads, realizing the gravity of implications that could be made from the last few sentences we've exchanged.

"Ready for the main course?" he asks, and I nod. Aaron walks around the table, grabbing my plate. "This is the best Valentine's Day ever," he whispers before placing the most tender kiss on the top of my head.

I have to agree seeing him reappear with the decanter in one hand and two plates balanced on his arm. "Thank you for making tonight so special."

He softly chuckles.

"What's so funny?"

"Are you calling it a night?"

"No. This is just so nice."

"Good. There's a lot of night left ahead ..." His words linger, and I am picking up what he is putting down. This is merely a prelude to a very, very sexy evening.

Cutting into his filet, a tension emerges on his face. "So ... remember our server from La Nonna?" he asks after a silent moment.

"Yes. How could I forget how much that girl was drooling over you?"

"She came into the bar the other day .... and was very flirty, grabbing my hand and everything."

"Okay? And?" *What is he getting at?*

"Being a bartender. I have to entertain a certain level of flirtation."

"What are you saying?" *Did he, like, kiss her or something?*

"I make six figures in a dive bar because the ladies love that I give them a little flirt. How do you feel about that?"

"Is that all you're giving them?"

He laughs. "That's all I'm giving them."

"Flirt away. Get that money!"

"Seriously, Sarah ... if we were together, would you want me to dial it back?"

If we were together ... Fuck. What if we were together? What if Aaron Olson was my boyfriend? I don't hate the idea. I actually really like it.

"Define how you're flirting with these ladies."

"Telling them they look nice. Listening to their stories. Remembering their dogs' names and important details they share with me ... generally being a nice guy that gives them attention."

"Aaron Olson. You are too cute. I thought you were going to say something far more scandalous."

"Like what?"

"Like ... I don't know ... like giving a little physical contact or something."

"Never. Well, I never initiate or reciprocate. Of course women grab my hand ... sometimes they even smack my ass as I walk past them."

"I understand why." I laugh. "Your ass is, like, the perfect muscle."

He smiles, then rubs the back of his neck. "I've never given out my number in the bar ... before you."

"Sure," I sass.

"You're the only one … I'm breaking all my rules with you."

I nod, taking a bite of my steak, feeling so full of the good kind of butterflies and from dinner.

"If we were together," I flirt. "I wouldn't be jealous because I would know that you're coming home to me … and I know you would be telling all of them to check out Main Street Makers Studio too."

28

Aaron

"I'll be your biggest promoter." I smile, happy she's cool with the part of my job that affords me my lifestyle.

Sarah Anderson could be my girlfriend if this night keeps going at its current pace. Now that would be something, having our anniversary be Valentine's Day.

"So, dessert. It's your time to shine, Sarah."

"Are you opposed to eating in the living room?"

"I am not," I say, clearing the table.

"Good." She stands. "Don't open the fridge."

"You're really building this up."

"Go sit in the living room."

I bite my lip, holding back from calling her bossy for a change. Sitting on the couch, my leg is bouncing up and down. This is that awkward transition from being respectful to mauling each other. I hope that's what she wants right now.

Sarah enters with the tray of chocolate covered strawberries and something behind her back. I love that she is so excited about whatever this surprise is. She places whatever it is on the side of the couch so I can't see and then puts the tray on the coffee table in front of me.

"Come here," I say after picking up one of the strawberries. She sits next to me, and I hold it in front of her mouth. She bites it, intentionally sexy. "Mmm," I hum. "That mouth."

She giggles, shielding her mouth as she chews. I pull her hand down, crashing my lips into hers. Sarah makes a little noise, and I stop.

"I'm still chewing!"

"And?" I breathe, cupping my hands on her jaw and going back in to kiss her. I taste the chocolate, the tartness of the berry, and the wine. I want to ... I need to know what she tastes like.

Pulling her on top of me, her short dress barely covers her ass, and I see a glimpse of pink underwear. "You look so fucking sexy in this dress," I breathe, running my hands up and down her legs.

"I should take my boots off," she softly says, straddling me.

I shake my head, grabbing the bottom of the dress. Slowly lifting it above her hips, I watch as she smiles, and I take that as a signal to take it all the way off.

"Fuck," I growl, seeing the matching pink bra and pantie set. Squeezing her hips, I rock them back and forth on me. "My Valentine," I breathe before kissing her chest and trailing my hands up her back.

"My surprise," she pants as my lips make their way to her neck. She leans over but can't reach the side of the couch. "Hold please." She giggles, dismounting from me.

"Whipped cream. What's that for?"

"Depends how creative you are," she says, grabbing

another chocolate covered strawberry and putting it to my lips.

"I have ideas," I say, before biting down. Holding eye contact with her, I grab the can from her, setting it next to me. "Get back here." I pull her back on top of me, kissing her collarbone, then the strap of her bra. She pulls my sweater off, and I toss it across the room.

"I've been thinking about licking these since the bar," she says, running her fingers down my abs.

"Give me these lips, sweetheart."

"Okay, Cherub," she sasses before wrapping her arms around my neck, and our tongues collide. The heat and intensity builds with every kiss. Lightly pulling my hair, she's quickly making me hard. I squeeze her breast, then her hip. She starts grinding on my hardness, rocking back and forth. My hands continue exploring. I squeeze her ass, and we're both breathing heavy. I pull her long brown hair, and she moans into my mouth.

As much as I want to rip her bra and underwear off of her body, we need to wait just a little bit longer.

"I want to feel how wet you are," I breathe, sliding my hand down her side and playing with the material at her hip.

"Who says I'm wet?" she challenges.

I look in her eyes, trailing my finger along the pink fabric before diving in. I huff, feeling her. "Exactly." Making slow circles on her clit with my thumb, I press two fingers inside of her. "Ride this hand. Show me how you're going to fuck me later."

"Aaron Olson," she breathes. "You are naughty."

"Be a good girl ... show me."

"I hate how much I like it when you say that."

"No you don't," I whisper in her ear, squeezing her ass with my available hand.

Sarah leans back, her hands gripping the back of my neck for leverage. Admiring her, I'm almost in disbelief watching her be completely in this moment with her eyes closed. Moving her hips in circles, she is fucking my hand just like I told her to. God she's hot when she listens.

"That's it, baby," I encourage. "Fuck this hand." She makes a small moan, and I love it. "Yes. I need to hear it. I need you to come."

Feeling her move up and down on my fingers, I am so turned on by how turned on she is. My thumb goes back to work on her clit, giving her extra sensation as she rides up and down. She whines, soft.

"Yes. Keep breathing. I want you to scream for me."

"I've never done this before," she pants. "I love it."

I love everything about this beautiful woman straddling me, riding my fingers. I admire her body move. "You're so sexy," just escapes my lips. She is too sexy. So fucking hot.

Tilting her head back, she stops riding.

"Tired?" I ask, picking up her slack and doing the work for her, fucking her with my fingers and keeping firm pressure on her clit.

She huffs a laugh, then breathes, "I'm so close."

I lightly wrap my hand around her neck, and Sarah reacts with a firm, "Yes. That." I squeeze, smirking at how we both like being a little rough.

"Come for me, baby," I whisper.

She moans, and I feel her pulse around my fingers. Taking them out, I lick them. "So sweet."

She rolls her eyes, and I toss her back on the couch. "Please hold," I tease, standing, having a very naughty idea pop into my head. "I'll be right back."

29

Sarah

"Where are you going?" I yell as I hear him walk up the stairs.

"One sec," he calls over his shoulder.

I bury my hands in my face, reliving how I just rode Aaron Olson's hand to orgasm. That was not on my 2025 Bingo Card. I giggle, loving it. I'm seriously loving every single thing about tonight so far.

"Oh my God!" I squeal, seeing him emerge with the angel wings on.

"Alexa, turn the lights red," he says, and the entire room goes red. I laugh while admiring his body in just jeans.

"What's in your hand?" I ask, seeing some kind of satin material.

"A tie."

"Oh?" I breathe, surprised and definitely turned on.

"Give me your wrists."

Yes, sir. I extend my hands, fucking giddy about whatever he has in mind.

"I'm feeling creative," he says, tying my wrists together.

"Are you?" I raise my brow.

"Lay on your back," he commands, grabbing the whipped cream.

To say I'm smirking is an understatement as I shimmy into a comfortable position on my back. Staring up at him, my buff fucking cherub, I love this unfolding fantasy. He shakes the can, and I bite my lip, my eyes darting from one of his muscles to another.

Aaron lifts my hands above my head. "Keep them there." His hand slowly trails down my arm, to my chest and then to my stomach.

"Or what?" I sass.

He sprays my neck, and I flinch at how cool it feels.

"Sarah," he breathes, shaking his head. "Do you play like this? Do you know what you're taunting?"

I laugh, nervous. "I'm punching above my weight class, I'm learning."

"Mmm," he responds, straddling me, not disagreeing.

Aaron Fucking Olson. So many surprises.

His tongue slowly and very deliberately licks the cream off my neck. Then he sprays my chest, slowly dragging his tongue to take all of it. His body scoots down before he sprays my lower stomach. Holding eye contact with me, he licks it, his tongue all the way out. What a fucking tongue ... long and thick.

"Aaron," I pant, so ready for that tongue to continue south.

"Lift your hips," he says, pulling down my underwear and putting it in his back pocket.

"Hey!"

"These are mine now."

"Such a thief!"

He chuckles then sprays the top of my pussy. I audibly breathe as he licks it off. Spraying my slit, I squirm before his tongue slowly licks and stays in place between my legs.

"Aaron," I breathe as his tongue teases.

Diligent. Detail oriented. Commanding. Adventurous. *He likes to please.* So many points for Aaron Olson. My first townie. *My last townie?* I wonder before that fucking tongue takes all of my attention.

"Just like that," I pant.

It's Valentine's Day, and a sexy ass angel is between my legs. *Role play.* This is something I need to do more ... a lot more, especially with Aaron.

"Aaron!" I moan, becoming overwhelmed at the way his tongue is going at me. His fingers hold me in place, not letting me squirm. He moves his hand to my low stomach, applying gentle pressure. "Fuck!" I whine. He knows exactly what he's doing.

"These noises. Keep making them," he says, muffled between my thighs.

Part of me wants to play with his hair, but what would happen if I disobeyed him? I'm getting the growing feeling that his kink level is off the fucking charts.

Fuck it. I get a hold of the can with my tied hands and squirt a line up my stomach. The noise makes his eyes look up at me. They're hungry, and he licks all of it up before he's hovering over me.

"You wanted my attention?" he growls.

"Let's go upstairs."

"I was in the middle of something."

"Sorry. I just ..."

"You wanted to be a brat. I know." He bites my shoulder hard, and I exhale loudly. "Don't test me again."

I run my tongue across my teeth, so badly wanting to say, *Or what?*

"Don't do it, brat," he breathes. "You might not like it."

I close my eyes, sticking out my tongue. "I think you're right," I barely whisper.

He grabs behind his back, pulling out my underwear, then shoves it in my mouth. "Now shut the fuck up so I can finish what I started."

I inhale sharply. Aaron Olson ... the dom ...

The girls are going to fucking die when they hear about this.

He grabs my legs, putting both of them over his shoulder, and then slams his tongue back into my clit. I moan upon contact, obsessed with this and every fucking detail of tonight.

His fingers squeeze my thighs before I feel two fingers enter me. Moaning, I am thrilled they've been added back into the equation. The licks, sucks, nibbles ... I'm on the edge, ready to come again for him. But then the rhythm of his fingers changes, going slower. The flicks of his tongue become delicate. *He's fucking dragging this out.* I moan in protest.

"A little longer, baby," he says, and I feel his breath on me.

I moan again, begging. He chuckles, then gets back to work. *Fuck.* I am going to explode. Lost in the sensations and the thrill, I shudder, my head jolting back, screaming into my gag.

30

Aaron

Hovering above her, I take her underwear out of her mouth, putting it back in my pocket.

"Oh my God," she whispers. "Um ... wow."

My face can't hide how much I like that she enjoyed it. Sitting next to her, I untie her wrists and place a soft, delicate kiss on her lips.

"Aaron ... you're a little freak!" She swats my arm, and I smile, taking another look at her in just a bra and boots.

"Sex in your thirties ... it hits different, right?"

"Aaron Olson hits different," she retorts. "I'm rarely speechless, and I am right now."

"So, you're having fun? You liked all of that?"

"Yes. I am having the best night of my life."

"Good." I play with the ends of her hair. "That's what I'm going for." I smile before we hold a heated stare.

"Take me upstairs already."

The list I'm building. If only she knew all of the punishments she would be getting ... if we were together like that. But we haven't talked about that. Hopefully this preview is enough to pique her curiosity.

"These wings. They have to stay on."

"I'll keep them on if you walk up the stairs very slowly and sexy."

"Easy enough." Sarah smirks before saying, "Alexa, play 'Love is a Bitch' by Two Feet."

I smirk, and she gets off the couch, so confidently swaying and making her way to the stairs. She smacks her ass, and I follow, obsessed. I let her stay a few steps ahead of me, loving her commitment to walking to the beat, teasing me, taunting me with her exposed ass and legs. Watching her, I am so ready to fuck her. She pauses, rubbing her hand up and down the banister. We both laugh. Then, she keeps going.

"The second door on the left," I say as she takes the last step up. In the doorway, she turns around, leaning on the doorframe. I unabashedly check all of her out. What a memory—her in a bra and over-the-knee boots with nothing else on.

"So, do you, like, want me to call you Daddy or something?" she asks, a bit of nervousness in her tone.

"Not tonight."

"Hmm," she responds in a high-pitched tone.

I grab her hips, pushing her backwards until she runs into my bed. "I want you to have fun."

"I'm having fun," she says, looking up at me. "Why is your bed so low to the floor?"

"I don't know. I like the look of it." I lean down, kissing her chest, then unclasp her bra. She leans her shoulders forward, and it falls to the floor.

"Another surprise." I chuckle, seeing a condom stuck to her nipple. I slowly peel the wrapper off her skin, then lick her nipple, putting the condom in my pocket. Grabbing both of her tits, I squeeze, moving my mouth from one to the next.

"Mmm," she breathes, her hand moving to my jeans, unbuttoning them. I quickly get out of them, and she sits on the bed, unzipping her boots.

"Did I say you could take those off?"

"I'm taking them off."

I chuckle, taking over, unzipping them and pulling them off. "If we ever do the Daddy thing, you are going to be punished for that smart mouth of yours."

"Talking a big game, Aaron Olson," she sasses, running her hands down my chest and stomach. Her hand dips below my briefs. "Fuck you," she softly says, the hunger in her eyes radiating through as she wraps her hand around my hard cock.

I bite my lip as she pulls my briefs down.

"Let's switch places. It's only fair that I take you to third base too."

Sitting on the edge of my bed with Sarah between my legs, I pull her in for a kiss first. "Confession," I whisper. "I wanted to ask you to homecoming senior year."

"What?! Why didn't you ask me?"

"You felt so out of my league."

"This dick is out of my league." She giggles before devouring it.

Fuck. She is just going for it. "You can take it," I pant, as her hand, mouth, and tongue are working so hard for me. "Look at you. You're so sexy," I say, sweeping her hair behind her shoulders. "This mouth … I'm going to come if you don't slow down."

She giggles, her mouth full of me. Taking that as a provocation, I guess, she takes all of me, bobbing up and down fast. "You made it disappear," I breathe, impressed.

"Fuck yeah. I can't wait to feel your pussy on this cock," I say, closing my eyes, leaning back onto my arms. The wings prevent me from really leaning back, and I chuckle at this fucking sight. I'd nearly forgotten about the wings. "When you fuck me, use me. Use your cherub however you want."

"Stop making me laugh," she says, her hand still stroking me.

We hold a smiley stare with each other before I ask, "Where do you want me to come?"

"I'll take it like a good girl," she says, her eyes blazing sex before she starts sucking me again.

I'm in love. I am never going to get enough of her. She's everything.

I buck up, on the edge, and she picks up her pace. "Yes, baby," I pant, releasing. "Take all of it."

Captivated, I admire her as she looks up at me. "The best girl," I praise, pulling her up and onto my lap. "These wings ... Do you want me to keep them on?"

31

Sarah

"The wings stay," I say, firm, loving how he is caressing my arms.

His mouth starts placing little kisses on my neck until his tongue trails along my collarbone.

"Goosebumps. Are you cold?"

"No." I smirk. "Just turned on."

"I don't believe you," he whispers. "Get under the covers."

"Alright, maybe I'm a little cold."

"Mmhmm."

He tucks me into the blankets, sitting next to my legs, looking at me thoughtfully. I can't help but giggle at the sight of him completely naked aside from a pair of fluffy angel wings. As he gently strokes my leg over the covers, I get the sense something is on his mind.

"What?"

He shakes his head.

"Tell me!"

"I know it's kinda fast but ... will you be my girlfriend?"

I put my hands on my cheeks, blushing, my heart racing

at this question. Aaron is such a romantic. Aaron is ... the perfect fucking guy.

"Yes."

"Yes?"

"Why wouldn't I want to be your girlfriend?"

He hovers over me, kissing me softly. "My Valentine." He winks, then kisses me with more passion. "Let me fuck my girlfriend," he breathes, pulling back the covers.

I want it so bad. I don't know if I've ever wanted it this bad. His fingers so gently run up and down my arm as we both stare at each other and the newness of this relationship. Aaron reaches across the bed, toward his nightstand.

"We ... don't need that," I softly say. He narrows his brow. "I'm your girlfriend."

"What about ...?"

"I'm clean and on the pill."

"Me too." He chuckles. "I mean, I'm clean. You sure?" he asks, and I nod. Then he bites his lip.

"Fuck your girlfriend already," I challenge, and his lips devour mine. His hands squeeze all over my body before he palms himself, putting the tip at my entrance. I softly smile, and he enters, slow. Aaron breathes, closing his eyes, feeling me.

"You're so perfect, Sarah." He leans down, placing the gentlest kiss on my lips before he starts slowly going in and out. I wrap my arms around his neck and my legs around his waist, wanting to be as close as possible to him.

"Little monkey," he chuckles and starts rubbing my clit as he thrusts faster. I close my eyes, giving in to every sensation, basking in the giddiness of Aaron being my boyfriend. My brain is so focused on him and everything he's doing to me. He's fucking me like I'm the main character. His lips and hands are just as busy as his cock.

"Tell me what you want."

"Break me."

He pulls out then flips me over, pulling my hips back. "You asked for it," he says before he's plowing into me, fucking trying to break my back as he thrusts into me. His cock has to be in my stomach.

"Yes," I pant, loving it.

"I'm so close," he pants. "I'm going to wait for you."

"I ... don't."

"That was with them. Not me."

I laugh in disagreement.

He bends down, speaking directly into my ear. "We're not going to sleep until you come on this cock."

"Yes, sir," instinctively comes out in response, and he smacks my ass.

"Now do as you're told," he says before kissing the back of my shoulders. He slows down, and his fingers return to my clit. The slow strokes and his lips on my neck are building me up. "Come for me," he breathes. "I've never wanted anything more. I want you to come on my cock. Give in."

I cry out, almost annoyed that he was able to ask for it and get it. Maybe all I ever needed was someone to speak this directly to me. Or maybe I just needed Aaron Olson.

32

Aaron

Placing baby kisses on her back, I'm euphoric. Her orgasm triggered mine, and now I'm basking in the afterglow. As I pull out, I can't believe this—how perfect we are together.

"Sarah Anderson," I finally say, "that was epic." I take off the angel wings and lie next to her, pulling her into my chest and kissing her forehead. "Let me grab you a warm washcloth."

She giggles. "I'm going to go pee."

I point toward the door connecting to the primary bathroom. She slips out of bed, and I open my dresser, grabbing a hoodie and sweatpants for her. I place them at the end of the bed.

"What's this?"

"For you, to be comfortable."

"I was going to sleep naked."

"I'm not going to argue with that. So, you're staying over?"

"How else am I going to fuck my boyfriend all night?"

"Come here," I say softly. She slides back under the

blankets, and I pull her in to be my little spoon, whispering in her ear, "My girlfriend."

"I would've said yes ... if you'd asked me to homecoming," she says, and I smile, kissing the back of her head. I couldn't be happier. Sarah rolls over, staring at me before whispering, "My boyfriend."

We both smile, and then she rolls on top of me. "Ready for round two?"

33

Sarah

Saturday, February 15th

Waking up next to Aaron, it feels so perfect. Watching my cherub sleep, it sets in that I have a boyfriend. My boyfriend is Aaron Olson. Who would have ever thought? I smile and throw on the hoodie. Making my way downstairs, I pick up some of the remnants from our evening—whipped cream and strawberries that got left out and various pieces of our clothing.

In the kitchen, I get coffee started for us, reliving the best Valentine's Day of my life. It sinks in that our anniversary will be Valentine's Day. *He's going to have to keep those wings.* I chuckle to myself. That can be our little tradition. The machine beeps, and I carry the two cups up to his room.

"No pants," he says, sitting up in bed. "My favorite."

"That reminds me." I chuckle. "I have to text my friends something."

Opening up the BFF group chat, I begin typing.

SARAH ANDERSON

In honor of this tradition we seem to be establishing ... Cupid shot ... a lot last night 🏔

RACHEL WAGNER

Of course he did!

EMILY BROWN

GTFO!

SARAH ANDERSON

He's also my boyfriend now so refrain from saying anything too raunchy.

RACHEL WAGNER

Goddammit! Now I'm the only single one!

EMILY BROWN

Nicholas has lots of ideas for St. Paddy's ...

SARAH ANDERSON

Are you feeling lucky, Rachel?

The End

Review Page

Do you want to help the author get more recognition?

Please review this book!

Review via: Goodreads.com

Or via your purchase platform!

About The Author

Writing under the pen name, Serena Pier is a wine lover, coffee snob & wife. With Midwestern roots, her stories are primarily set in and around Chicago. Serena is deeply fascinated by power dynamics; her stories always explore unequal social status.

Thank you for reading Cupid's Shot: A High Five Novella. It's the second in a series of three holiday-themed novellas featuring friends Emily, Sarah, and Rachel.

Check out Serena's other books at www.SerenaPier.com.

Follow Serena Pier on TikTok and Instagram: @SerenaPierWrites